Tales from the
Arabian Nights

Tales from the Arabian Nights

Retold by Stephanie Laslett
Illustrated by Helen Cockburn

P
· PARRAGON ·

A Parragon Book

Published by
Parragon
13 Whiteladies Road, Clifton, Bristol BS8 1PB

Produced by
The Templar Company plc,
Pippbrook Mill, London Road, Dorking,
Surrey RH4 1JE

Printed and bound in China.
ISBN 0 75252 598 0

Contents

HISTORY

The three stories in this book belong to one of the greatest story collections of all time, *The Tales of the Arabian Nights,* which were first heard many hundreds of years ago.

First translated into French by Antoine Galland at the beginning of the 18th century, they were originally told by the beautiful Princess Scheherezade to the suspicious Prince of Tartary, who had threatened to behead her at daybreak. But her tales were so exciting that, as the sun rose, he longed to hear how they ended and so pardoned her life for one more day, until after one thousand and one nights Scheherezade had won his trust and his heart.

Aladdin
and the
Magic Lamp

Once upon a time in far-off China there lived a poor tailor called Mustapha. He struggled hard to support his wife and his only son, Aladdin, but there was never enough money and they were often hungry. Mustapha wanted Aladdin to learn a trade and become a tailor like himself, but the boy was lazy and ran off whenever his father called.

After a time, Aladdin's idle ways made Mustapha so unhappy that he fell ill and died.

Then Aladdin grew even more disobedient. He was never to be found at home with his mother but was always running around the streets of the town with his friends.

One day when he was playing in the streets as usual, a stranger came up and spoke to him.

"Are you the son of Mustapha the tailor?" he asked.

"I am, sir," replied Aladdin, "but he died a long while ago."

At this the stranger hugged and kissed him. "I am your uncle," he said. "I recognised you because you look just like your father. Run and tell your mother I am coming."

Aladdin ran home and told his mother the news.

"Indeed, child," she said,

"your father did have a brother, but I always thought he was dead." What she didn't know was that this was no uncle, but instead a cunning magician.

She hurried to prepare their supper, and Aladdin ran off eagerly to fetch their guest, who came laden with fruit and wine.

"Do not be surprised that we have never met before," he said to Aladdin's trusting mother, "for I have been on my travels for forty years."

He then asked Aladdin which trade he had learned. Ashamed,

the boy hung his head and his unhappy mother burst into tears. When the magician heard that Aladdin was idle and would learn no trade, he offered to buy a shop for him and stock it with fine goods.

Next day the magician bought
Aladdin a new suit of clothes
and took him all over the city,
showing him the sights. He
brought him home at nightfall
to his mother, who was overjoyed
to see her son looking so grand.

The following day the magician took Aladdin for a walk beyond the city gates. After a while, they sat down by a fountain and the magician pulled a cake from his pocket and divided it between them.

Then they journeyed onwards until they almost reached the mountains. Aladdin was so tired that he begged to go back, but the magician kept him amused with pleasant stories, and led him on for many more miles.

At last they came to two mountains divided by a narrow valley.

"We will go no further," said the false uncle. "Now I will show you something wonderful. Quickly gather up some sticks so I can make a fire."

When it was lit the magician took some powder from his pocket and, throwing it on the flames, muttered a strange magic spell. The earth trembled and then opened up in front of them to reveal a flat square stone with a brass ring in the

middle. Aladdin was dreadfully
afraid and tried to run away,
but the magician caught him
and gave him a blow that
knocked him to the ground.

"What have I done, uncle?" he
whimpered. "Don't be afraid,"
replied the magician more
kindly, "but you must obey me.
Beneath this stone lies a treasure
which will be yours, and no-one
else may touch it — but you
must do exactly as I tell you."

At the word "treasure", Aladdin
forgot his fears and did as he
was bid! He grasped the ring

and heaved with all his strength. To his astonishment, the stone came up quite easily and he could see steps leading down into a dark cave.

"Go down," said the magician. "At the foot of these steps you will find an open door leading into three large rooms. These rooms lead into a garden of fine fruit trees. Walk on until you come to a stone wall. Look for a hole in the wall and there you will find a lamp. Bring it to me carefully and we will both be exceedingly rich."

The magician drew a ring from his finger and gave it to Aladdin, saying, "This will protect you. Now go safely and do as you have been told!"

Aladdin found everything just as the magician had said. The trees in the garden were laden with strange fruit which sparkled and gleamed in the light.

"How my mother would love to see these," he thought, and quickly filled his pockets to overflowing. Soon he had found the lamp and returned to the mouth of the cave.

Hopping with impatience, the magician cried out,

"Hurry and give me the lamp!"

But Aladdin was on his guard. He was afraid of his new uncle and feared he might be left underground forever.

"No!" he cried. "First you must

help me out of the cave."

At this the magician flew into a terrible rage, for now his evil plans had been completely ruined. Some years ago, he had read in his magic books about a wonderful lamp which would make him the most powerful

man in the world. After careful study, he had worked out where it was hidden, but there was a problem. He could not fetch the lamp himself. Someone else would have to find it and bring it to him. He had picked out Aladdin for this purpose, thinking him to be a foolish good-for-nothing. He pretended to be the boy's uncle to gain his trust, but once he had the lamp, he intended to leave Aladdin in the cave forever.

Now his plot had failed and with a loud curse, the magician

threw some more powder on the fire and the stone rolled back into its place with a dreadful boom! The wicked magician fled far away to Africa, leaving Aladdin trapped in the dark cave.

For two whole days Aladdin wept bitterly. Finally, he fell on his knees and prayed to God for mercy. As he clasped his hands, he accidentally rubbed the ring which the magician had given him. With a rumble and a flash, a huge genie rose out of the ground in front of the startled Aladdin.

The boy fell flat on his face and trembled with fear in front of the terrifying figure.

"What is your wish?" thundered the genie. "I am the Slave of the Ring and will obey you in all things."

At this, Aladdin lifted his head and begged, "Free me from this place!" At once the earth opened, and he found himself outside — but where was the genie? Dazed and confused, Aladdin trudged home. His poor mother was frantic with worry. Her son explained what had happened, and showed her the lamp and the fruits he had gathered in the garden.

"My son, these are not fruits but precious jewels!" she cried, holding them up to the light. "But what is this old thing?" and she picked up the lamp. "Maybe if it was clean we could sell it," she said and began polishing it.

Flash! An enormous genie appeared and bowed low. Aladdin's mother fainted with surprise, but Aladdin quickly snatched the lamp and said boldly:

"Fetch me something to eat!"

Soon the genie returned. He carried twelve silver plates piled high with rich food and on his head he balanced two silver cups of wine.

And so they feasted while Aladdin told his mother about the lamp. She begged him to sell it, and have nothing to do with the genie. "No," said Aladdin. "Good luck has given this magic lamp and ring to me and I am not afraid to use them."

From then on, Aladdin sold the silver plates one by one, until he had spent all the money they

fetched. Then he summoned
the genie once again, requested
another set of plates, and thus
they lived for many months.

Now the king of this country
was a mighty Sultan, rich and
powerful. He had a beautiful
daughter who loved to bathe
in the springs of a garden nearby.
The Sultan had ordered that on
these days everyone was to stay
home and close their shutters
for it was forbidden to look at
the Princess as she passed by.
But Aladdin was filled with a
desire to see her face.

He hid himself behind the garden door and peeped through a chink. The Princess lifted her veil as she went inside and looked so beautiful that Aladdin fell in love with her at first sight.

He went home and told his mother that he loved the Princess so deeply that he could not live without her, and meant to ask the Sultan, her father, for her hand in marriage. His mother burst out laughing. "The Princess would never marry *you*!" she said. "She will want to marry a Prince!"

But at last Aladdin persuaded her to visit the Sultan with his request. Then his mother remembered the magic fruits. "I will take these as a gift to the Sultan," she decided, wrapping

them in a cloth. The poor woman
was nervous as she entered the
great hall of the palace. Seated
at the far end was the Sultan,
with his chief minister, the Grand
Vizir, and all his lords and
courtiers. Many loyal subjects
had come to speak to the Sultan
and the old woman had to wait
her turn. At last, she found
herself kneeling before him.

"Forgive me, your Majesty," she
begged, "for I come with an
impudent request. Aladdin, my
son, has fallen in love with your
daughter and wishes to marry

her. In vain have I prayed that he might forget her. Now I have done as he asked and beg forgiveness, both for my son and myself." Slowly, she unfolded the cloth and there lay the jewels in all their beauty.

The Sultan was thunderstruck. He turned to the Grand Vizir and said,

"Surely this young man deserves the Princess if he values her at such a high price."

But the Grand Vizir was most displeased. He wanted the Princess to marry his own son.

"Haven't you heard?" was the answer. "The son of the Grand Vizir is to marry the Sultan's daughter tonight."

Breathlessly, she ran and told Aladdin, who at first was overwhelmed with grief. But then he thought of the lamp. He rubbed it, and the genie appeared, saying, "What is your will?"

Aladdin replied, "The Sultan has broken his promise to me, and the Grand Vizir's son is to marry the princess. I command you to bring both of them here to me tonight, before the wedding."

He begged the Sultan to wait for three months, hoping that in this time his son would be able to find a richer present. The Sultan agreed and told Aladdin's mother that although he gave permission for the marriage, she must now wait for three months. Aladdin was overjoyed to hear the news and waited patiently.

After two months had passed, his mother went into the city one day to buy cooking oil and found everyone rejoicing. She asked what was going on.

"Master, I obey," said the genie, and that night he returned with the terrified Princess and her husband-to-be.

"Lock up this man," ordered Aladdin, pointing to the Grand Vizir's son. As soon as he was alone with the Princess he spoke gently.

"Fear not, dear Princess. I only wish to save you from a marriage that should not be. Your father promised you to me if I could wait three months."

But the Princess was too frightened to speak, and passed the most miserable night of her life. In the morning, the genie fetched the shivering prisoner and carried him and the Princess back to the Palace.

Soon the Sultan and his wife came to wish their daughter good morning. But the Princess trembled and shook and would not say a word. Her father grew angry and demanded to hear the truth so at last the Princess sighed deeply and told them all that had happened the night before.

The miserable son of the Grand Vizir also admitted the truth.

"I dearly love the Princess," he added, "but I would rather die than go through another such fearful night. Break off the marriage, I beg you!"

And so the wedding was cancelled, and all the feasting and rejoicing came to an end.

Once three months had passed, Aladdin sent his mother to the palace to remind the Sultan of his promise. When he saw the old woman, the Sultan was most anxious to save his daughter from marrying into such a poor family. He turned to the Grand Vizir for advice.

"Ask Aladdin to pay such a high price for the Princess that he will never be able to afford it," whispered the crafty Grand Vizir.

And so the Sultan turned to Aladdin's mother. "Good woman,

a Sultan must remember his promises, and I will remember mine. But your son must first send me forty basins of gold, brimful with jewels, carried by forty slaves. And all of them must be splendidly dressed. Tell him that I await his answer."

With that, Aladdin's mother bowed low and went home, thinking all was lost.

But Aladdin summoned the genie, and in a few moments the forty slaves arrived, and filled the small house and garden to overflowing.

The magnificent procession entered the palace, led by Aladdin's mother. The slaves bowed low before the Sultan, and delivered their gifts at his feet.

The Sultan was lost for words at the sight of such splendour. When at last he could speak, he turned to the old woman.

"Good woman, return and tell your son that I wait for him with open arms." Soon Aladdin was busy preparing for the wedding. With a quick polish of the lamp, he called for the genie.

"I want some fine silk clothes,

a magnificent horse and ten
thousand pieces of gold in ten
purses."

No sooner had he said it, than
it was done. Aladdin looked so
handsome that even his own
mother had some difficulty
recognising him.

"Now we must build a palace fit for the Princess," he said to the genie. "Build it of the finest marble, set with jasper, agate, and other precious stones. In the middle, build me a large hall with walls of gold and silver. Around each window I want a border of diamonds, rubies and emeralds. There shall be fine stables for my horses and a magnificent garden with crystal-clear fountains and sweet-smelling flowers for my dear Princess. Go and see to it at once!"

Aladdin's splendid new palace was finished the next day, and everyone was astounded by its magnificence. Soon it was time for the wedding. Loud cheers filled the air as Aladdin and his mother arrived at the Sultan's Palace.

Cymbals clashed and a fanfare of trumpets rang out as the Sultan came out on to the steps to welcome them both. The Princess was well pleased by the sight of the handsome Aladdin and that night she said good-bye to her father, and set out for her new home.

"Princess," said Aladdin, "you have only your beauty to blame if my boldness displeases you."

But the Princess was far from angry. She was happy to obey her father and so the marriage took place with much rejoicing and merriment.

Aladdin's gentle nature soon won the hearts of the people. He was made Captain of the Sultan's armies, and won several battles for him, but the Grand Vizir remained suspicious, believing in his heart of hearts that Aladdin was a magician.

And so Aladdin and his Princess lived in peace and contentment for several years.

But far away in Africa the magician was brooding about the magic lamp. By his magic arts, he discovered that Aladdin, instead of perishing miserably in the cave, had escaped, and had married a Princess with whom he was living in great honour and wealth. He knew that the poor tailor's son could only have accomplished this with the help of the lamp, so he travelled night and day until he

reached the capital of China,
determined to bring about
Aladdin's ruin. As he passed
through the town he heard
people talking about a marvellous
palace with gilded walls and
jewelled windows.

"Forgive my ignorance," he asked them, "but what is this palace you speak of?"

"Have you not heard of Prince Aladdin's palace?" was the reply. "It is the greatest wonder of the world!"

Soon the magician had found the palace and straightaway guessed what had happened.

"That lamp will be mine!" he fumed, half-mad with rage, "and once again Aladdin shall live in deepest poverty."

The magician schemed and plotted and bided his time. Soon his chance came. Aladdin was leaving on a hunting trip and would be away all day. The magician bought a dozen copper lamps, put them into a basket, and hurried to the palace gates. "I will give new lamps for old!" he cried and it was such a strange offer that a jeering crowd soon followed him.

The Princess was curious and sent her servant to find out what the noise was about.

"Madam," she said, "outside there is an old fool offering to exchange fine new lamps for old ones."

The Princess laughed also and catching sight of the magic lamp on the high shelf, and knowing nothing of its power, said, "Why, there is an old lamp. Take that and fetch me a new one."

The magician nearly shouted for joy when he saw that his plan had worked. Quickly he snatched the magic lamp and, thrusting his basket at the puzzled servant girl, hurried out of the city gates to a remote hillside, where he remained until nightfall. Then he pulled out the lamp and rubbed it. With a flash, the genie appeared.

"Your wish is my command, oh, master," he said, bowing low. Clapping his hands with glee, the magician ordered the genie to carry him, together with the palace and the Princess, back to his home in Africa.

Next morning the Sultan looked out of the window towards Aladdin's palace and rubbed his eyes, for it was gone! He sent for the Grand Vizir, and he, too, was astonished.

"But I have long feared something such as this," he told the Sultan. "I believe Aladdin is a magician and has cast this spell on the Princess."

The Sultan sent thirty men on horseback to capture Aladdin.

They met him riding home from the hunt. Quickly they bound him in chains and forced him to go with them on foot. But the townspeople loved Aladdin and were determined to see that he came to no harm. They followed behind, carrying swords and cudgels. Aladdin was carried before the Sultan, who ordered the executioner to cut off his head. The executioner

made Aladdin kneel down,
blindfolded him, then raised his
huge, curved scimitar in the air.
  But at that very moment the
Grand Vizir saw that the crowd
had forced their way into the
courtyard and were scaling the

walls to rescue their favourite Prince. The Sultan could see that his people would never forgive him if he went ahead with the execution so he ordered the executioner to put down his sword and Aladdin was unbound.

Still the crowd looked threatening so in a loud voice the Sultan announced that Aladdin would be granted a Royal Pardon. His life was safe.

Aladdin now begged to know what he had done.

"You wretched trickster!" said the Sultan. "Come over here," and he pointed to the empty space where his palace had once stood.

Aladdin was so amazed to see that his palace was gone that he was completely lost for words.

"Where is my daughter?" demanded the enraged Sultan. "I can accept the loss of the palace, but you must find my beloved daughter or you will lose your head."

Aladdin fell to his knees.

"The Princess means more to me than life itself," he cried. "Give me forty days and I will find her. If I should fail, then I will return and suffer my punishment."

For the next few days Aladdin wandered about like a madman. He had lost everything — his palace, his Princess and his magic lamp.

"What am I to do?" he wailed as he tramped the streets of the town. He asked everyone he met if they knew what had become of his palace, but they only laughed and felt sorry for him.

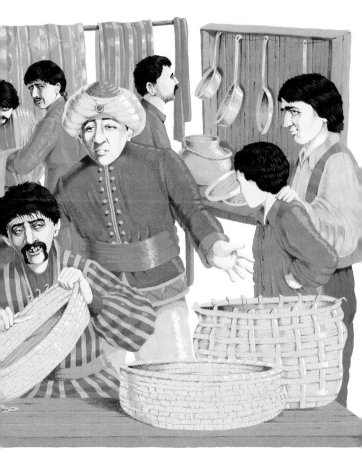

He came to the banks of a river and, feeling quite desperate, decided to throw himself in and end his sorrows. But as he clasped his hands to say his last prayers, he rubbed the magic ring he still wore on his finger.

Instantly, the genie appeared. "What is your wish, oh, master?" he boomed.

"Save my life, genie," said Aladdin, "and bring my palace back from wherever it has gone."

"That is not in my power," said the genie. "I am only the Slave of the Ring — you must ask the Genie of the Lamp."

"Very well," said Aladdin, "Take me to the palace instead, and set me down under my dear wife's window."

No sooner had he said this than he found himself in Africa, under the window of the Princess where he fell asleep out of sheer exhaustion.

He was awakened by the singing of the birds, and for some time sat wondering what to do. He realised that all his bad luck was due to the loss of the lamp, and tried in vain to think who could have stolen it.

That morning the Princess rose early. As she dressed, she listened to the birdsong outside her window.

"How I wish I was as free as a bird," she said. "I should fly like an arrow to my dear Aladdin and leave this wretched place forever."

The magician would not let her out of the palace. Each day he visited her room and with honeyed words would try to win her love. She dreaded his knock at the door and would have forbidden him enter if she could.

With a deep sigh the Princess sat down and her maid began to brush her long hair. Suddenly the maid stopped. She had seen someone hiding outside. Quickly the Princess ran to the window and opened it wide. There stood Aladdin, and great was their joy at seeing each other again.

After they had kissed, Aladdin said, "Dear Princess, before we speak of anything else, you must quickly tell me what has become of the old lamp I left on a high shelf in the hall of our palace!"

"Alas!" she said. "It was me who caused all our sorrows for I did not know the lamp was a magic lamp. An old man came to the palace, calling 'New lamps for old!' I spied your dusty old lamp lying on the shelf and thought we had no further use for it. My maid took it outside and when she returned with a nice, new lamp I was well pleased. Oh, forgive me, Aladdin, forgive me!"

Then Aladdin understood all that happened. The Genie of the Lamp had a new master.

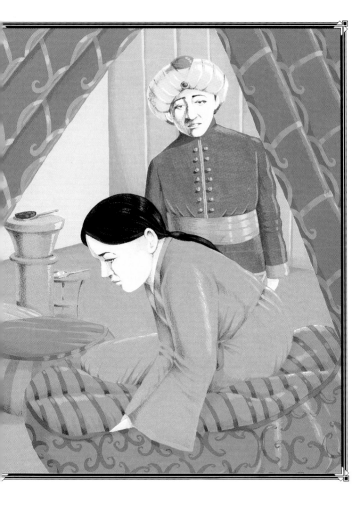

"Now I know who is really to blame!" cried Aladdin. "That old man was the evil magician! Quick, tell me! Where is the lamp?"

"He carries it with him all the time," said the Princess. "Once he pulled it out of his robe and showed it to me. He told me that you were beheaded on my father's orders and now he wants me to marry him. He is for ever speaking ill of you, but I can only reply with my tears."

Aladdin comforted her, and then left her for a while.

He thought long and hard and finally devised a clever plan. He visited the apothecary and bought a special powder, then returned to the Princess who let him in by a little side door.

"Put on your most beautiful dress," he told her, "and receive the magician with smiles. Make him believe that you have forgotten me. Invite him to dine with you, and say you wish to taste the wine of his country. He will go to fetch some, and while he is gone this is what you must do."

She listened carefully to Aladdin"s
plan and, after he had gone,
she dressed herself in her finery
for the first time since she left
China. She put on a necklace
and head-dress of diamonds
and as she looked in her

mirror she could see that she looked more beautiful than ever. Then she invited the magician to visit and soon he arrived at her door. She welcomed him inside with smiles and sweet words.

"I have made up my mind that Aladdin is dead, and that all my tears will not bring him back," she explained to the astonished magician. "I will mourn no more, and have therefore invited you to dine with me. But I am tired of the wines of China, and would like to taste those of Africa."

The magician bowed low to the Princess, then hurried down to the cellar to select the finest of African wines. While he was gone, the Princess put her hand in her pocket and pulled out the powder which Aladdin had given her.

Quickly she poured it into her cup. When the magician returned, he served the wine. The Princess asked him to drink her health, and handed him her cup in exchange for his as a sign of friendship.

Before the toast, the magician made a speech in praise of her beauty, but the Princess cut him short, saying

"Let us drink first, and you shall say what you will afterwards." She held her cup to her lips and watched as the magician lifted his wine and swallowed every last drop. Slowly his eyes widened in horror and he clutched at his throat. "I have been poisoned!" he gasped and with a loud groan the magician fell lifeless to the floor.

Crying with relief, the Princess opened the door to Aladdin, and flung her arms around his neck. Then Aladdin went to the dead magician, took the lamp out of his robe and commanded the genie to carry the palace and all inside back to China once again.

The Sultan sat all alone in his room, mourning his lost daughter. For the hundredth time that day he looked out of the window to the spot where Aladdin's palace used to be. Suddenly he jumped to his feet and rubbed his eyes, for there stood the palace, exactly the same as before!

The Sultan ran up the marble steps and was overjoyed to find his precious daughter safe and well. Angrily, he turned to Aladdin and demanded to hear the truth.

"My story is true, for I could never trick your Majesty," said Aladdin. "This evil magician spirited away your daughter but now he is dead and we can all live in peace ever more."

The Sultan was so delighted by their return that he ordered

of ten days feasting and after this Aladdin and his wife did indeed live in peace in their beautiful palace. When the Sultan died, Aladdin took his place and reigned for many years, leaving behind him a long line of just and beloved kings.

Ali Baba
and the
Forty Thieves

In a town in Persia there lived two brothers, one named Cassim, the other Ali Baba.

Cassim was married to a rich wife and lived in a fine house with plenty to eat and drink. His brother, Ali Baba, was very poor and looked after his wife and children by cutting wood in a nearby forest and selling it in the town.

One day, when Ali Baba was working in the forest, he saw a troop of men on horseback coming towards him in a cloud of dust. He was afraid they were robbers and climbed into a tree for safety.

Soon they were passing beneath him and, to his surprise, they pulled up their horses and dismounted. Ali Baba counted forty men.

The finest man among them, whom Ali Baba took to be their Captain, went a little way among some bushes, and said "Open, Sesame!" so clearly that Ali Baba heard him.

A door in the rocks swung slowly open, and the Captain ordered his troop of men to go in. Then he followed and the door closed behind them.

They stayed inside some time and Ali Baba, fearing they might come out and catch him, was forced to sit patiently in the tree.

At last the door opened again. The Captain came out, and watched carefully as his Forty Thieves passed by him. Then he closed the door, saying "Shut, Sesame!"

Each man mounted his horse and off they galloped

into the distance with a great thundering of hooves. Then Ali Baba climbed down and went to the secret door hidden behind the bushes. "Open, Sesame!" he cried, and the door flew open. Ali Baba expected to see a dark, dismal hole but he was greatly surprised to find a large cave with a hole in the roof to let the light in.

The cave was full of treasure. Before him lay great heaps of silver and gold, carpets of velvet and silk and bags overflowing with coins.

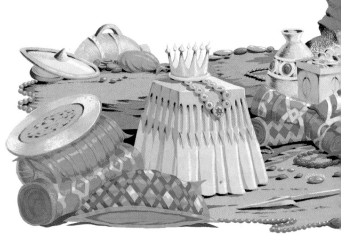

Ali Baba entered the cave and the door shut behind him. He went straight for the gold and picked up as many bags as he thought his asses could carry.

Quickly he loaded his animals with the gold, and then hid the treasure beneath bundles of sticks.

"Shut, Sesame!" said Ali Baba. The door closed and he went home.

Ali Baba drove his asses into the yard, shut the gates and carried the money bags to his wife.

"We must keep this secret," he told her. "I will bury the gold in the garden."

"First let me measure it," said his wife. "I will borrow a measuring jar from someone while you dig the hole."

So she ran to the wife of

Cassim and borrowed a measuring jar. Knowing Ali Baba was poor, Cassim's wife was curious to find out what sort of grain Ali Baba wished to measure, and so she put some lard in the bottom of the jar.

Ali Baba's wife went home and measured the gold. Over and over again she filled, then emptied the jar. How happy she was!

But when she returned the jar, she did not notice that a piece of gold was stuck to the lard in the bottom.

As soon as she had left, Cassim's wife spotted the gold and she grew very curious. When Cassim came home she said:

"Cassim, your brother is richer than you. He does not count his money — he *measures* it."

He begged her to explain this riddle, which she did by showing him the piece of money and telling him where she found it. Then Cassim grew so envious that he could not sleep.

Before sunrise next morning he visited his brother. "Ali Baba," he said, showing him the gold piece, "you pretend to be poor and yet you are measuring gold." Ali Baba realised that thanks to his wife's foolishness, Cassim and his wife had discovered their secret. Straightaway he confessed what he had done and offered Cassim a share of the money.

"Of course I shall have a share," said Cassim, angrily, "but I must know where the treasure is hidden, or there will be trouble!"

Ali Baba, more out of kindness than fear, told him about the cave, and the exact words to use.

So Cassim left Ali Baba. He intended to cheat him and get all the treasure for himself. He rose early next morning and set out with ten mules loaded with great chests. He soon found the place, and the secret door in the rock.

"Open, Sesame!" he cried and the door opened and shut behind him. He could have feasted his eyes all day on the treasures, but quickly he began to gather together as much as he could carry.

But when he was ready to go he was so busy thinking about his great riches that he could not remember what to say. Instead of "Sesame," he said "Open, Barley!" and the door remained fast. He named several different sorts of grain, all but the right one, and the door still stuck fast. He was so frightened of the danger he was in that the word went right out of his head.

About noon the robbers returned to their cave, and saw Cassim's mules roving about with great chests on their backs. Someone was stealing their treasure!

Quickly they drew their sabres and surrounded the cave. "Open, Sesame!" cried the Captain and the door swung open.

Cassim heard the trampling of their horses' feet and was determined not to die without a fight, so when the door opened he jumped out and threw the Captain down. In vain, however, for the robbers with their sabres soon killed him.

Then the thieves saw Cassim's bags laid ready, and they could not imagine how anyone had got in without knowing their secret. They cut Cassim's body into four quarters, and nailed them up inside the cave, in order to frighten anyone else who might venture inside, then off they went in search of more treasure.

As night drew on Cassim's wife grew very anxious. She ran to her brother-in-law, and told him where her husband had gone.

Ali Baba comforted her and then set out for the forest with his asses in search of Cassim. The first thing he saw on entering the cave was his dead brother.

Full of horror, he laid the body on one of his asses, and the bags of gold on the other two and, covering everything with bundles of sticks, he returned home.

He drove the asses laden with gold into his own yard, and led the other to Cassim's house. The door was opened by the slave Morgiana, whom he knew to be brave and cunning.

Unloading the ass, he said to her, "This is the body of your master. He has been murdered, but we must bury him as though he had died peacefully in his bed. I will speak with you again, but now go and tell your mistress that I have arrived."

When Cassim's wife heard the terrible news of her husband's death, she began to wail and cry. So Ali Baba offered to take her to live with him and his wife.

"But you must promise to follow my advice and leave everything to Morgiana," he said. Gladly Cassim's wife agreed, and she dried her eyes.

Meanwhile, Morgiana had

thought of a plan. She visited an apothecary and bought some pills. "My poor master can neither eat nor speak," she said, "and no-one knows what ails him." She returned home with the pills, but went back the next day.

"He is worse," she wept. "I need the strongest medicine you have, for I fear that he will die."

That evening no-one was surprised to hear the wretched shrieks and cries of Cassim's wife and Morgiana, telling everyone that Cassim was dead.

Early the next day, Morgiana went to an old cobbler near the gates of the town. She put a piece of gold in his hand, and told him she had some work for him to do.

She blindfolded him with a scarf, then led him to the room where Cassim's body lay. She removed the old man's blindfold and asked him to sew the four quarters together. The poor cobbler did as he was told and then, with his eyes covered, he was led back to his home.

Then they buried Cassim, and Morgiana followed him to the grave, weeping and tearing her hair, while Cassim's wife stayed at home and wept bitter tears. Next day she went to live with Ali Baba, who gave Cassim's shop to his eldest son.

When the Forty Thieves returned to the cave, they were astonished to find that Cassim's body had gone and yet more of their moneybags were missing.

"We are certainly discovered," said the Captain, "and shall be undone if we cannot find out who it is that knows our secret. Two men must have known it; we have killed one, we must now find the other.

"I need one bold and cunning robber to go into the city dressed as a traveller and discover whom we have killed, and

whether there is talk about the manner of his death. If this messenger fails he must lose his life, for we could all be betrayed by him."

One of the thieves jumped up and offered to do it, and, as the other robbers praised him for his bravery, he disguised himself.

At daybreak he entered the town, close by the stall of Baba Mustapha, the cobbler. The thief wished him good-day, saying,

"Old man, how can you possibly see to stitch at your great age?"

"Old as I am," replied the cobbler, "I have very good eyes. Believe me when I tell you that only recently I sewed a dead body together in a place where I had less light than I have now."

The robber was overjoyed at his good fortune and, giving the cobbler a piece of gold, asked to be shown the house where he had stitched up the dead body.

At first Mustapha refused, saying that he had been blindfolded, but when the robber gave him another piece of gold he began to think he might remember the way if he was blindfolded just as before.

The plan succeeded, for the robber partly led the cobbler, and was partly guided by him, right to the front of Cassim's house.

The robber marked the door with a piece of chalk. Then, well pleased, he said farewell to Baba Mustapha and returned to the forest.

By-and-by Morgiana saw the mark the robber had made, and quickly guessed that some mischief was brewing. She fetched a piece of chalk and marked two or three doors along the street with a similar cross, without saying anything to her master or mistress.

The thief, meantime, was busy telling the other robbers of his discovery.

The Captain thanked him, and wanted to see the house he had marked. But when they came to it, they saw that five or six other houses were chalked in the same manner.

The robber was so confused that he was lost for words, and when they returned he was at once beheaded for having failed. Another robber was sent off and, having once again bribed Baba Mustapha to show him the way, he marked the door with red chalk, but Morgiana was still too clever for them and so a second robber was also put to death.

The Captain now decided to go himself but, wiser than the rest, he did not mark the house, but looked at it so closely that he could not fail to remember it.

He returned, and ordered his men to go into the neighbouring villages and buy nineteen mules and thirty-eight leather jars, all empty, except for one, which was full of oil.

The Captain put one of his men, fully armed, into each jar. Then he rubbed the jars with grease so they looked as if they were full of oil.

Then the nineteen mules were loaded with thirty-seven robbers in jars, and the jar of oil, and they reached the town by dusk. The Captain stopped his mules in front of Ali Baba's house, and said to Ali Baba, who was sitting outside in the cool, "I have carried this oil a long way to sell at tomorrow's market, but it is now so late that I know not where to stay the night, unless you will do me a favour and take me in."

Though Ali Baba had seen the Captain of the robbers in the forest, he did not recognise him in the disguise of an oil merchant. He wished him welcome, opened his gates for the mules to enter, and told Morgiana to prepare a bed and supper for his guest.

He brought the stranger into his home, and after they had eaten, Ali Baba went again to speak to Morgiana in the kitchen. Meanwhile the Captain went to the yard, pretending to look after his mules, but really to instruct his men.

Beginning at the first jar and ending at the last, he said to each man, "As soon as I throw some stones from the window of my bedroom, jump out of the jars, and I will be with you in a trice."

He returned to the house, and Morgiana led him to his bedroom. She then asked Abdallah, a slave like herself, to help her make some broth in a pot for their master. But as they set to work, the lamp in the kitchen went out.

"We have no more oil left in the house," said Abdallah, "but there is plenty of oil in those jars outside. Why not go and help yourself?" Morgiana agreed this was a good idea and, taking his oil pot, she went into the yard.

When she got close to the first jar, she was amazed to hear a voice from inside ask her softly, "Is it time?"

Now, any other slave but Morgiana would have screamed and run away. But Morgiana, realising immediately what was afoot, answered quietly, "Not yet, but soon."

Then she visited all the other jars, one by one.

And hearing the same question from each, she gave the same answer until she came to the jar of oil.

Realising that her master had been tricked by the oil merchant into allowing thirty-eight robbers into his house, she filled her oil pot and lit her kitchen lamp. Then she went back to the oil jar and filled her largest pan.

She boiled the oil on her fire then poured enough oil into every jar to stifle and kill the robber inside.

When this brave deed was done she went back to the kitchen, put out the fire and the lamp, and waited to see what would happen.

In a quarter of an hour the Captain of the robbers awoke, got up, and opened the window. As all seemed quiet he threw down some little pebbles which hit the jars. He listened, and as none of his men seemed to stir he grew uneasy, and went down into the yard.

He went to the first jar and said, "Are you asleep?" But when he smelt the hot boiled oil, he knew at once that his plot to murder Ali Baba and his household had been discovered.

The Captain soon found that all of his gang were dead and, seeing his oil jar empty, he guessed how they had died.

In a fearsome rage, he broke down the garden door and, climbing over several walls, made his escape. Morgiana heard and saw all this, and, rejoicing at her success, went to bed and fell asleep.

At daybreak Ali Baba arose, and, seeing the oil jars still there, asked what had happened.

Morgiana told him to look in the first jar and see if there was any oil. When he saw that instead of oil there was a man, he started back in terror.

"Have no fear," said Morgiana. "The man cannot harm you for he is dead."

When Ali Baba had recovered somewhat from his astonishment, he asked Morgiana what had become of the oil merchant.

"Merchant!" said Morgiana, "He is no more a merchant than I am!" and she told Ali Baba all that had happened, assuring him that the plot had failed and now there was only one robber left.

At once Ali Baba gave Morgiana her freedom, for he owed her his life. They then buried the robbers in Ali Baba's garden, and sold their mules in the market.

Meanwhile, the Captain returned to his lonely cave. Without his companions to share the wealth, it now seemed a terrible place. He resolved to avenge them by killing Ali Baba.

He disguised himself as a
merchant, and went into
the town, where he took
lodgings at an inn. He
visited the cave many

times and carried away
many rich materials and
much fine linen, and set up
a shop opposite that of Ali
Baba's son.

He called himself Cogia Hassan and, as he was both polite and well-dressed, he soon made friends with Ali Baba's son and, through him, with Ali Baba whom he often asked to dinner.

Ali Baba, wishing to return the merchant's kindness, invited him to his own house. He welcomed him with a smile and thanked him for his kindness to his son. When the merchant was about to take his leave Ali Baba stopped him and asked, "Where are you going, sir, in such haste? Will you not stay and sup with me?" The merchant refused, saying that he had a reason and, when Ali Baba asked him what that was, he replied, "It is, sir, that I can eat no food that has salt in it."

"If that is all," said Ali Baba, "let me tell you that there shall be no salt in either the meat or the bread that we eat tonight."

He went to give this order to Morgiana, who was much surprised. "Who is this man," she said, "who eats no salt with his meat?"

"He is an honest man, Morgiana," replied her master, "therefore do as I tell you." But Morgiana was curious to see this strange visitor, so she helped Abdallah carry up the dishes. She saw in a moment that Cogia Hassan was the robber Captain and that he carried a dagger under his coat. "I am not surprised," she said to herself, "that this wicked man, who intends to kill my master, will eat no salt with him. Only friends share salt with their food and he is no friend; but I will soon spoil his scheming."

She sent up the supper with Abdallah, while she prepared the bravest of plans. When the dessert had been served, Cogia Hassan was left alone with

Ali Baba and his son. His evil plot was to make them both drunk and then murder them.

In the meantime Morgiana put on a head-dress like a dancing-girl's, and fastened a belt round her waist, from which hung a dagger with a silver hilt.

"Take your tabor, Abdallah," she said, "and let us go and entertain our master."

So Abdallah obediently went to find his small drum and when they arrived at their master's door Morgiana made a low curtsey.

"Come in, Morgiana," said Ali Baba. "Let Cogia Hassan see your fine dancing."

Now Cogia Hassan was by no means pleased, for he feared that his chance of killing Ali Baba was gone for the present, but he pretended to be glad to see Morgiana, and Abdallah began to play and Morgiana started to dance.

After she had performed several dances she drew her dagger and made passes with it, sometimes pointing it at herself and sometimes at her guests, as if it were part of the dance. Suddenly, out of breath, she snatched the tabor from Abdallah with her left hand and, holding the dagger in her right, held out the tabor to her master. Ali Baba and his son each put a piece of gold into it, as was the custom.

Cogia Hassan, seeing that she was coming to him, pulled out his purse. But while his hands were busy, Morgiana plunged the dagger into his heart.

"Wretched girl!" cried Ali Baba in astonishment. "Whatever you have done will surely ruin us!"

"I did this to *save* you, master, not to ruin you," answered Morgiana.

"See here," she said, opening the false merchant's coat and showing the dagger that he had been hiding. "See what an enemy you have been entertaining! Look at him! He is both the false oil merchant and the Captain of the Forty Thieves."

Ali Baba was so grateful to Morgiana for thus saving his life that he offered her to his son in marriage, for they had long been in love. And a few days later the wedding was celebrated with great splendour.

After the feasting was over, Ali Baba at last set off for the cave.

"Open, Sesame!" he cried, and the door flew open at

once. In went Ali Baba and saw that all the treasure was still there. He brought away as much gold as he could carry, and returned to town, a rich man.

In time, he told his son the secret of the cave, which his son handed down in his turn, so the children and grandchildren of Ali Baba were rich for the rest of their lives.

Sinbad
the Sailor

This is the story of Sinbad the Sailor and some of his strange adventures at sea. He travelled far and wide and each new voyage brought danger and excitement, as you will see!

His first voyage was on a merchant ship bound for the East Indies. It passed many islands along the way and stopped to trade with the natives. One day the ship was becalmed near a strange little island quite unlike any land the sailors had ever seen before. It was smooth and green and lay quite flat in the sea. The captain gave the crew permission to go ashore and soon they were stretching their legs on dry land. The cook had lit a fire and was preparing to make a meal when suddenly the island began to tremble and shake. The sailors still on board cried out in a panic.

"Quick! Run for your lives!" they shouted. "The island is moving!" But it was not an island after all. They had landed on the back of a whale and the heat of the flames had made him very cross indeed!

Quickly the sailors ran for safety, some scrambling into the sloop and some swimming straight for the ship. The captain raised his sail and as soon as most of his sailors were aboard, the ship weighed anchor and was gone. But Sinbad was left behind, struggling in the swirling sea as the great whale dived out of sight. He clung to a piece of driftwood and prayed to Allah to save him from the dangers of the deep. Soon darkness fell and Sinbad passed the terrible night in a daze.

Early the next morning Sinbad's prayers were answered for as the sun rose above the horizon he could see an island — a real island — and as the sun moved across the sky, the waves pushed him closer and closer to land until eventually he was thrown exhausted upon the beach.

This island was blessed with sweet spring water and plentiful fruit and so Sinbad survived for several days. But as time passed he feared he might never be rescued and would be doomed to spend the rest of his days lost and alone.

One day he resolved to explore the island fully and climbing to the top of a tall tree he scanned the island for signs of life. At first he could see nothing but sky, sea, sand and mile after mile of green forest but then his eye was caught by something white in the distance. Scrambling down from the tree he set off in the direction of this strange object. When he got close he saw it was a huge white dome, perfectly smooth but with no door or windows.

As Sinbad stared at it in wonderment, the sky suddenly grew dark and, lifting his head, he saw an enormous bird flying overhead. It was a Roc and the terrified sailor recalled how he had heard that this bird was so large that it fed its young on elephants!

The bird alighted upon the dome and Sinbad realised that it was her egg! As the Roc slept Sinbad had an idea.

"Maybe this Roc can help me escape from the island," he thought to himself and, unwrapping the turban from around his head, he tied himself securely to the bird's foot. All night long he waited for the bird to awake and at dawn she stood up and with a great cry took off into the sky. Higher and higher she soared, then suddenly swooped down and landed far below.

Hastily Sinbad untied himself and looked about. He was in a deep rocky valley surrounded on all sides by mountains.

"I will never escape from this dreadful place," he wailed. "Would that I had stayed on the island where there was at least food and drink to sustain me!" With a heavy heart he began to walk but had not gone far when he spotted something glistening on the ground. Bending down, he found to his amazement that the earth was studded with hundreds of glittering diamonds.

But as he admired their beauty, he saw something which struck fear into his heart. Watching him from the caves high above were many huge serpents, each one large enough to swallow an elephant in one go. They hid from the Rocs during the day and did not leave their caves, but at night they came down to catch what food they could find.

As the sun began to sink, Sinbad desperately searched for a place to hide. The serpents hissed loudly as they slithered down the valley towards him.

Quaking with fear, Sinbad crawled into a small hole and blocked the entrance with a rock. The terrible snakes hissed at him but could do him no harm. He was safe.

At sunrise the serpents slowly returned to their caves and Sinbad scrambled from his hole. As he stretched his cramped limbs, a huge piece of meat came crashing to the ground behind him. Down came another, and another. Then Sinbad remembered a story he had heard about diamond hunters. There was no way into the Valley of Diamonds and so they had devised a trick to bring the diamonds out. They threw lumps of meat down from the mountains onto the valley floor. The diamonds stuck to the moist flesh. Then eagles would swoop upon the meat and carry it to their nests in the mountains. Here the men lay in wait and, as soon as the birds had landed, they scared them away with sticks and could then safely pick the jewels from the meat. Sinbad realised the eagles could carry him out of the valley too.

Quickly he gathered as many diamonds as his pockets could carry and, once again untying his turban, he bound himself to the largest piece of meat and lay flat on the ground.

Straightaway an enormous eagle seized the meat with his talons and Sinbad found himself lifted into the air. The bird soared to the summit of a mountain and alighted on her nest. All at once a great hue and cry broke out and a man leapt out from behind a rock, waving a large stick. The frightened eagle dropped the meat and Sinbad speedily freed himself.

"What magic trickery is this?" cried the man when he saw a man but no diamonds. Then Sinbad described all that passed.

When Sinbad offered to share his own diamonds between them the man was most friendly and soon they were travelling to the city to exchange their gems for gold and silver.

After this, Sinbad returned home to Baghdad and great was the welcome, for his family had given him up for dead. So he passed several months in luxury and wanted for nothing, but after a time he longed for adventure once again. So, bidding his family farewell, he set sail on a merchant ship bound for distant shores.

"Allah preserve us!" cried the captain and he fell to his knees on the deck. "That is the Island of the Ape Men. They are fearsome beasts and there wil! be no escape once they lay hands on us!"

Sure enough, Sinbad could see the creatures, half man, half ape, jumping up and down upon the shore. Suddenly they began swimming towards the ship and were soon crawling onto the decks and swarming up the rigging. They were covered with thick red hair and their eyes shone like yellow jewels.

The journey passed well enough for several months. The ship dropped anchor in the harbours of many fine cities and her merchant passengers did good trade and were well pleased. But their good luck was soon to end for one day a violent storm descended upon them and the tempestuous seas threatened to engulf them at any second. A great wind blew up and drove them off course and, when the gale had moved on, they could see an island rearing out of the sea straight ahead of them.

The creatures could only
grunt and bark and, as the
captain beat his breast and
cried aloud, they cut through
the ship's ropes and cables
with their sharp teeth.

When they were close to land, the Ape Men forced every sailor and merchant to swim ashore and, as Sinbad looked back, he was aghast to see that the wicked creatures had taken the ship and were quickly sailing away!

There was nothing for it but to explore the island and look for food and water. After many hours in the blistering heat they came upon a magnificent palace with high walls and tall spires. The huge ebony gates were ajar and so the exhausted group of men went inside,

hoping to find kind hospitality.
But the place seemed quite
empty and deserted. Fires
burnt under roasting spits in
the courtyard and to one side
was a huge mound of what
looked suspiciously like
human bones! The men were
too tired to take another step
so they sat down and rested.
Suddenly the earth trembled
and a dreadful roar filled the air.

A huge ogre lumbered through
the gates and towered over the
terrified men. So horrible was
the sight that most of them
fainted clean away on the spot.

The giant had one burning red
eye in the middle of his
forehead. His teeth were long
and very sharp and his bottom
lip hung down like a camel's.
He had huge elephant ears and
talons like an eagle. He was
hideous.

When Sinbad came to, the first thing he saw was the ogre's huge eye just inches away from his face. To his great fear, he realised that the beast had him in his hand and was pinching him with two leathery fingers. The giant's fetid breath swept over him and Sinbad could hardly breathe. Then, with a short grunt of disgust, the ogre dropped Sinbad to the ground and picked up the captain. This time he let out a long rumble of pleasure, for the captain was nice and plump! He would have this one for his supper.

Soon the poor man was being roasted on a spit and as the others looked on in horror, the ogre ate him and tossed his bones on top of the large pile in the corner of the courtyard. Then, with much smacking of lips, the giant lay down on his back and slept, snoring loudly all the while.

The frightened men huddled together and spoke in whispers.

"We must escape!" said one.

"We must kill him!" said another, but no-one could agree on a plan.

"Listen to me," said Sinbad.

"We must make rafts and keep them on the shore so if we do not manage to kill the ogre then we at least have some means of escape off the island."

So it was agreed and they set to work immediately. The next evening the ogre once again picked a plump sailor for his supper but as he slept the men took two red-hot iron spits and thrust them into his one eye. With a great howl, the beast leapt to his feet and staggered out of the courtyard.

"He is not dead!" cried Sinbad. "To the rafts, to the rafts!"

They ran to the beach as fast as their legs could carry them and hastily pushed their flimsy rafts into the water. But who was this charging through the wood after them? It was the ogre — but he was not alone. He was accompanied by his wife, a giantess even more hideous than her mate. Roaring angrily, she picked up huge boulders as if they were pebbles and threw them into the sea, capsizing several rafts in one go. Soon the only sailors left alive were Sinbad and two companions.

The sea tossed them like a straw all through that dreadful night and the wretched men feared they would die at any time. But as the sun rose in the east they spied land and to their great joy the waves eventually threw them upon a sandy beach.

After walking some way, they congratulated themselves on their good fortune at having landed on an island with sweet water and ripe fruit and soon they were much restored in spirit and in health.

That night the three men slept upon the beach but were

wakened by a rustling sound coming towards them. Suddenly a great serpent reared over them and, darting forward, caught one of the sailors and swallowed him down. Sinbad and his one remaining companion quickly scuttled for safety.

"What misfortune is this!" wailed Sinbad. "We have escaped the cruelty of an ogre and the raging seas only to face this new and even more terrible danger." All that night the two men sat and shook but saw no more of the awful serpent. The following night they climbed into a tree.

"We will be safe from harm up here," decided Sinbad, but as the darkness gathered they could hear the serpent rustling towards them and with a great surge, he reared up from the ground and snatched Sinbad's companion from his branch.

The poor sailor was swallowed at once and the serpent slid away. Sinbad clung to the tree and trembled all through that long night.

The next morning he gathered as much dry wood as he could find and made himself a circle of small fires completely surrounding the tree. That night the serpent arrived as before but this time the flames kept him at bay. All night he lay in wait like a cat watching a mouse but at sunrise the hungry beast slunk away and Sinbad was safe once more.

The exhausted Sinbad could not face the prospect of another such night and so he ran to the beach, resolving to throw himself headlong into the sea and end all his troubles. But imagine his surprise and delight on seeing a ship pass by at that very moment! Unwinding his turban, he waved the bright cloth in the air and shouted at the top of his voice. Soon, to his great delight, the sailors had spotted him and turned the ship around. As Sinbad climbed aboard, the crew flocked about him, eager to hear his story.

They could hardly believe
their ears when they heard that
he had successfully escaped the
dreaded cannibal ogre and his
wife, not to mention the fearsome
serpent. The captain welcomed
him on board the ship and soon
he had been fed and dressed in
new clothes. As Sinbad rested,
he overheard the captain giving
instructions to one of the crew.

"When we disembark at our
next port," he said, "be sure you
do not unload these goods, for
they belong to a sailor called
Sinbad who we lost at sea many
weeks ago. A huge whale has

most likely swallowed him, but I wish to return his belongings to his bereaved family."

Then Sinbad leapt from his bed and hailed the captain. "It is I, Sinbad!" he cried. "Do you not recognise me? It was I who was left behind on that whale that we mistook for an island!" Then the captain embraced him and showed him the goods that he had kept safe and sound. And when they called at the next port, Sinbad increased his riches with wise purchases of cloves, cinnamon and other spices.

As they finally sailed for home they saw many wonders such as a tortoise twenty yards in length and a fish which looked like a cow and gave milk to its young.

And so after many months, Sinbad returned home, a prosperous merchant laden with fine goods, and his family were overjoyed to see him for they had long given him up for dead.

For several months Sinbad enjoyed the security and comforts of home, but as time passed, curiosity stirred within him and he longed to sail the high seas once again. Soon he was on board a merchant ship headed for the eastern isles with a fair wind in its sails. After a long, long voyage the ship finally arrived at a small island.

The ship's provisions were almost gone and the sailors and merchants had a fearsome hunger so the first thing they looked for was something to eat. Soon one of them gave a great cry. He had discovered a Roc's egg, similar in size to the one Sinbad had discovered on a previous voyage. As the crew gathered round, they could hear a faint tapping sound. Suddenly a crack rent the egg from top to bottom and the young Roc's bill appeared. Sinbad begged them not to touch the egg for he remembered the size of the mother Roc he had met before, and he feared they would be in grave danger if she returned, but the famished crew would not listen. Eagerly, the sailors attacked the shell and soon had the young Roc roasted upon a spit which they set up on the shore.

They fell on the meat like wolves as Sinbad sat to one side and watched them. Suddenly, he felt a shadow passing over him. Looking up, he saw the mother Roc flying high overhead, and close behind flew the enormous father Roc.

"Run for the boats!" cried the captain when he realised the danger they were in, and as the sailors scrambled hand over hand up the ropes, the ship set sail. Meanwhile the two Rocs had discovered their broken egg and no infant remaining. With anguished cries, they wheeled around and headed after the ship.

High overhead the Rocs circled and the sailors cowered beneath them on deck. Suddenly the huge birds flew off back to the island and a great shout of relief went up from the crew. But their joy was shortlived for soon the Rocs returned and this time each clasped a huge boulder in its talons.

With a triumphant scream, the Rocs dropped their burdens and they landed so exactly on the middle of the ship that it broke into a thousand pieces and every man on board was thrown into the sea.

Once again, poor Sinbad found himself clutching a spar of wood and counting himself lucky that he had not joined many of his shipmates who now lay at the bottom of the sea. One by one his companions drowned and Sinbad was the only survivor of that dreadful attack. Good luck continued to smile on him that day for soon a favourable wind got up and blew him towards a nearby island and as he lay gasping for breath on the sandy beach he gave thanks to Allah for saving his life once more.

This island too was blessed

with ripe fruit and pure water and soon Sinbad was much recovered in body and in spirit. He began to explore inland but had not gone far when he saw an old, old man, very weak and feeble, sitting by a brook.

"Hello, there," called Sinbad. "What country is this?" He got no reply from the old man who simply shook his head in a sorrowful fashion. After a while he raised his head and indicated that he wished Sinbad to carry him on his back over the brook so that he could gather fruit from the trees on the far side.

This Sinbad did gladly, for he was ever willing to help others less fortunate than himself. But when he got to the other side and bent down so that the man could step off his back, the old man simply gripped even tighter with his legs. He wrapped them so strongly around Sinbad's neck that he passed out and fell to the ground. Then the old man, whom Sinbad had thought so weak and sickly, gave him a mighty kick in the ribs and forced poor Sinbad to stumble to his feet and continue walking with the man still on his back.

And so poor Sinbad was little more than a beast of burden as the old man directed him from tree to tree. Steadily his new master ate his way through fruit after fruit and when night fell, the two slept locked together, with the old man's legs still gripped fast about Sinbad's neck.

In the morning, the bad-tempered old man kicked Sinbad awake and so the day's toil began again. Thus the week passed and poor Sinbad was desperate to rid himself of this troublesome burden. How he wished he had never stopped to do this good deed but he had no time to dwell on the matter for as soon as his steps faltered, the old man set about his head with his hands and there was no escaping his ill humour.

One day Sinbad spied a pile of empty gourds on the ground. While the old man slept, he carefully picked up a gourd, squeezed a quantity of grape juice into it and left it lying in the sun for several days. When he next returned to that place, he tasted the wine he had made and found it to be good and strong.

Soon he had a new spring in his step and his burden did not seem quite so heavy.

The miserable old man noticed the change in Sinbad's spirits at once and demanded to know what was in the gourd.

"It is wine, old man," replied Sinbad. "It gives me new strength and vigour." Then the old man was eager to taste it and Sinbad handed him the gourd. The old fool drank deep and soon he was dancing on Sinbad's shoulders and singing at the top of his voice. Needless to say, it wasn't long before he fell off!

Sinbad spotted his chance at once and took to his heels. Loudly the old man wailed as he realised the mistake he had made but Sinbad did not even look back over his shoulder.

Once again he roamed the shore, scanning the far horizon for a passing ship, and once again he was in luck. A heavily laden merchant ship picked him up and when they heard of his account of the old man, the sailors clapped him on the back.

"You had a lucky escape," the captain cried. "That is the old man of the sea and many men

have died in his service. You are
the first to ever escape his
clutches."

So Sinbad was safe once more
and after a good meal and the
gift of some new clothes, he felt
much restored. After some days
had passed, a merchant on
board the ship invited Sinbad to
accompany him on a trip to a
neighbouring island renowned
for its coconuts. Each carrying a
large bag, they set off for a
grove of straight, tall trees with
bark so smooth it was
impossible for any man to climb
up and reach their fruits.

The palm trees were alive with monkeys who chattered angrily at Sinbad far below. He was told to gather stones and then watched in amazement as the merchant threw the rocks at the monkeys. The creatures became incensed and grabbed the nearest missiles to hand — the coconuts. Soon coconuts were raining down around them and Sinbad quickly filled his bag.

This plan proved so effective that Sinbad eventually amassed a great pile of coconuts with which to trade at different ports. At each place they disembarked, he headed straight for the market and bartered for pepper and wood of aloes.

At one island he was shown the largest and most lustrous pearls he had ever seen. Hiring his own divers, he sat and watched while they fetched him shell after shell, each one concealing a hidden treasure.

So he returned home with more bounty and more tales to tell.

This time Sinbad rested for a full year before embarking once again on an adventure. He left a distant sea-port with a captain bound on a long voyage but after many weeks at sea the mariner declared that they were lost. Anxiously the crew scanned the horizon and when at last land was sighted, they were confounded by their captain's reaction. He fell to his knees, tore off his turban and beat his breast, calling loudly to Allah to save them all from the dreadful fate that surely awaited them.

"That is the most treacherous coastline in the whole of the Persian Gulf!" he cried. "We are caught in a rapid current and will be dashed upon the rocks. We are doomed, doomed!" Sure enough, the sailors seemed powerless to steer the ship away from the shore and soon the vessel ran aground and was broken into many pieces. The desperate sailors rescued what they could but were dismayed to find signs of many previous shipwrecks all along the coast. There was indeed no escape and one by one the men died.

Sinbad was the last to succumb to starvation and in desperation he hunted for a means of escape. He noticed that a channel of the sea ran some way inland and then disappeared underground.

"I shall follow its course," decided Sinbad, and he made a small raft. Carefully lashing his goods to the wooden spars, he climbed aboard and resigned himself to the will of Allah.

The current swept him along and soon the raft entered a dark cave. Sinbad lost all track of time as the hours passed in total darkness and silence.

The roof of the cave grew closer and closer and eventually Sinbad had to lie flat to avoid knocking his head on the overhanging rocks. As he lay tightly clinging to his goods, sleep overcame him and he knew no more.

When at last he awoke he was delighted to find that his surroundings had quite changed, for he was now amongst lush green fields. But then he saw that his raft had been moored against the river's edge and a group of natives stood watching him warily from the bank. None seemed able to understand him and at last in desperation Sinbad recited an Arabic prayer.

"Call upon the Almighty and he will help you. Shut your eyes and whilst you sleep, God will change your bad fortune into good." On hearing this, one of the men spoke out and welcomed Sinbad to their land. They offered him gifts of food and as he ate, he recounted the story of his voyage. They were most impressed and eager for him to repeat his story to their King at his palace in the city.

As Sinbad entered the city of Serendib, for that was its name, the people gathered around, curious to see this visitor to their small island.

He approached the King and bowing low before him, kissed the ground.

"My name is Sinbad," he said, "and I come from Baghdad." The King wished to know how he had arrived on the island of Serendib, and then Sinbad told the tale of all his voyages. The King was so entertained that he commanded that the adventures be written in letters of gold on vellum and kept forever in his library. Then Sinbad presented him with gifts from the goods he had rescued on his raft, and the King was well pleased by his generosity.

"You must take back a present from Serendib for your Sultan," decided the King and he dictated a letter to accompany the gift.

"To the Sultan, from the King of the Indies, before whom march a hundred elephants and whose palace shines with a hundred thousand rubies and twenty thousand diamond crowns."

When the time came for Sinbad to leave, the King came in great procession to the harbour to say farewell. He rode upon a magnificent elephant. A palace guard walked in front of him, carrying a long golden lance, and another guard stood upon the elephant's broad back and carried a huge green emerald upon a red velvet cushion.

And so Sinbad set sail for his own country and as soon as he arrived in Baghdad, he went to the Sultan's palace to present the King of Serendib's letter and his gifts. The Sultan was much impressed by the generous presents, among which was a single ruby carved into a cup about six inches high and filled to the top with perfect pearls; a snake skin which had the power

to heal anyone who lay down upon it; bountiful quantities of wood of aloes and camphor; and a beautiful slave whose dress was covered in jewels. "I must reply to the King at once," declared the Sultan. "Sinbad, you will return to him with gifts from Baghdad."

Poor Sinbad had been hoping to spend some time recovering from his latest voyage but the Sultan would brook no delay and so a ship was loaded with costly presents from Arabia and Sinbad set course for the Island of Serendib.

Many days later he landed safely at the harbour, far away from the treacherous coast where he had been shipwrecked some months before. The King of Serendib welcomed Sinbad and was well pleased with the presents sent by the Sultan of Arabia. Happily he admired the beautiful coat made of gold cloth, fifty robes of rich brocade, yard upon yard of finest white linen, the magnificent carved table and the crimson velvet bed and at last he declared himself a great friend of the Sultan.

His task completed, Sinbad once again bade farewell to the Island of Serendib and set sail for home, but, alas, his journey was not to be a happy one. Four days from Serendib the crew were attacked by pirates and captured as slaves. On arrival at a neighbouring island, each rich merchant was stripped of his clothing and dressed in shabby rags, then sold to the highest bidder. Sinbad was bought by a local merchant who, luckily for him, treated him well. One day he called Sinbad to his side.

"Today you will go and shoot

elephants for me. Take this bow
and arrow and do not return
until you have killed at least one."

Then Sinbad was taken to a
forest and made to climb a tree
and lie in wait for the elephants
to pass by. He spent the night
without sleep but it was not
until sunrise that the great
beasts arrived. To Sinbad's great
dismay, they sensed his
presence and, surrounding the
tree, stared at him with such
malevolence that he almost fell
from the tree in fright. Then the
largest beast wrapped his trunk
around the tree and pulled hard.

The tree toppled to the ground and Sinbad fell with it. He was plucked up by the elephant and slung on his back and, more dead than alive, was carried off to a low hill. There the animal left him alone and when Sinbad drew strength enough to look around he could see he was surrounded by the bones and tusks of countless elephants.

Sinbad knew at once that this was the elephants' own burial ground; the place they would come to when it was time for them to die. He realised that these wise animals had brought him here to show him that elephants should be allowed to die in their own time and not be hunted and killed simply for the ivory in their tusks.

Straightaway he returned to the merchant's house and explained what he had seen. When the merchant saw with his own eyes the remains of the hundreds of elephants who had died upon the hill, he was sombre.

"This is indeed an awesome sight," he told Sinbad. "I will take what ivory I can carry from this place and swear that I will hunt them no more." And so Sinbad loaded the elephant upon which they had come with many long tusks and then they returned to the merchant's house. The merchant was well pleased with Sinbad and as a mark of his appreciation he declared that he was no longer a slave but from henceforth could go free.

And so Sinbad returned home on his final voyage, for from that time on he never went to sea again. He had had great adventures and escaped danger and death more times that he cared to remember. He had survived mountainous seas, deadly rocks, hideous serpents and ogres, pirate attacks and all manner of strange afflictions. Now he wished to spend the rest of his days in the safe harbour of his house, tended by loving family and friends. After twenty seven years of travelling, Sinbad was home at last.